This Book belongs to :

_____

_____

Let's Play
I Spy

I spy with my little eye
something beginning with letter....

A Is for

Accordion!

I spy with my little eye
something beginning with letter....

B Is for

Bagpipe

B Is for

Beard

I spy with my little eye
something beginning with letter....

B Is for

Boot

I spy with my little eye something beginning with letter....

B Is for

Bow Tie

C Is for Clover

I spy with my little eye something beginning with letter....

C Is for

Coins

I spy with my little eye something beginning with letter....

C Is for

Cupcake

I spy with my little eye
something beginning with letter....

D Is for

Dog

I spy with my little eye
something beginning with letter....

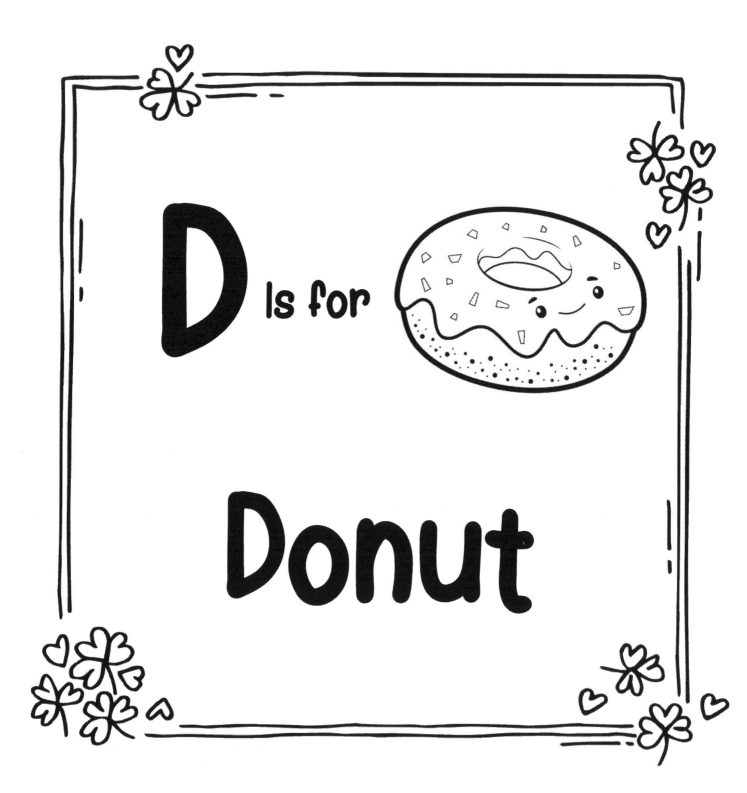

D Is for Donut

I spy with my little eye
something beginning with letter....

E

Is for

Elephant

I spy with my little eye something beginning with letter....

F Is for

Flag

I spy with my little eye
something beginning with letter....

G Is for

Gnome

I spy with my little eye
something beginning with letter....

H Is for

Harp

I spy with my little eye
something beginning with letter....

H Is for

Hat

I spy with my little eye
something beginning with letter....

H

Is for

Horseshoe

I spy with my little eye
something beginning with letter....

i Is for

ice cream

I spy with my little eye
something beginning with letter....

J Is for

jar

I spy with my little eye
something beginning with letter....

K Is for

Kite

I spy with my little eye
something beginning with letter....

K Is for

Kiwi

I spy with my little eye something beginning with letter....

L

Is for

Lollipop

I spy with my little eye
something beginning with letter....

L

Is for

Leprechaun

I spy with my little eye
something beginning with letter....

M Is for

Mug

I spy with my little eye
something beginning with letter....

N Is for Necklace

I spy with my little eye something beginning with letter....

O Is for

Owl

I spy with my little eye
something beginning with letter....

P

P

Is for

Pillow

I spy with my little eye something beginning with letter....

P Is for

Pot of Gold

I spy with my little eye
something beginning with letter....

Q Is for

Quiche

I spy with my little eye something beginning with letter....

R

Is for

Rainbow

I spy with my little eye
something beginning with letter....

R

Is for

Ring

I spy with my little eye something beginning with letter....

S Is for

Scarf

I spy with my little eye
something beginning with letter....

S Is for

Shamrock

I spy with my little eye something beginning with letter....

S Is for

Sock

I spy with my little eye
something beginning with letter....

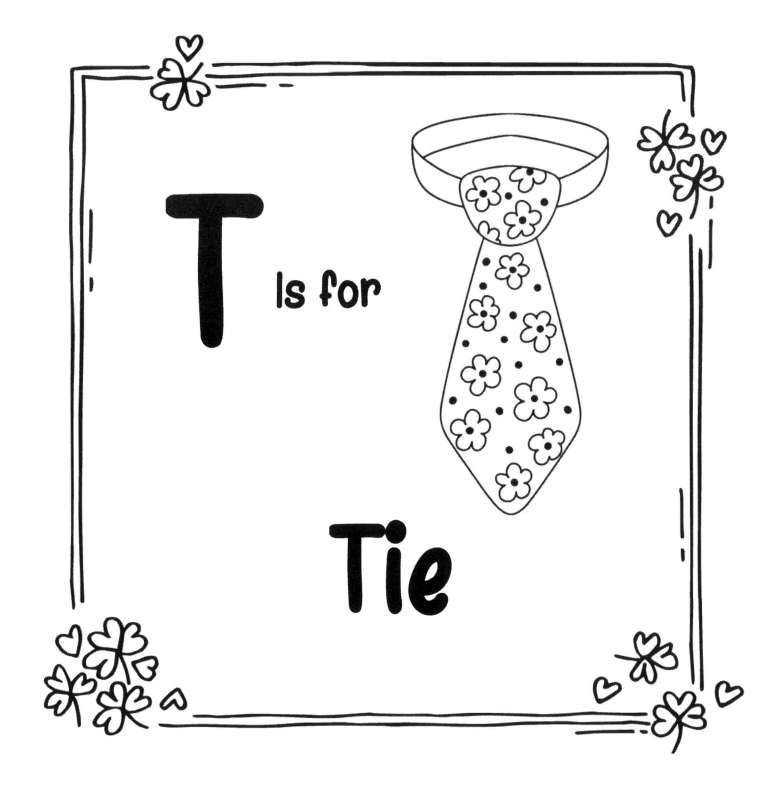

T

Is for

Tie

I spy with my little eye something beginning with letter....

U Is for Umbrella

I spy with my little eye something beginning with letter....

U Is for

Unicorn

I spy with my little eye
something beginning with letter....

I spy with my little eye
something beginning with letter....

W Is for

wreath

I spy with my little eye something beginning with letter....

I spy with my little eye something beginning with letter....

Y Is for

Yarn

I spy with my little eye
something beginning with letter....

Z Is for

zebra

Made in the USA
Las Vegas, NV
05 March 2024

86702063R00048